Hangin' With Mimi!

by Sally North

Can't wait to see you again!

We have so much fun
hanging out together!

Hangin' out with Mimi
is a special kind of fun.

We do all kinds of crazy things...

like dancing in the sun!

Sometimes we chase the butterflies,

and run around the park.

Or hide beneath the blankets...

when it's really, really dark.

Sometimes we
bake some cookies...

or some other crazy food.

We act a little silly...

'cause we're in a happy mood!

Sometimes when
I'm at Mimi's place,

I play with lots of toys.

And then she reads a book to me,
and I don't make a noise.

Sometimes we do some shopping
at the big, amazing mall.

Or play a little tennis...

or go play a little ball.

Then when it's time for me to leave,
she hugs me really tight.

And says,
"Good-bye,
I love you,
see you later
and good night."

Hangin' With Mimi!

Sally was born in Jackson, Michigan. She has lived all over the country with her husband, Fred. They have 3 grown children, and they all live in Louisville, KY. She has written over 30 children's books and had her first book published in 2000. Sneaky Snail Stories are all sweet and simple rhyming books with really cute illustrations. You can see all the Sneaky Snail Stories at: www. sneakysnailstories.com

Other books by Sally:

No Pancakes for Puppy
Grandma and Grandpa Love Me
No Cookies for Kitty
My Aunt Loves Me
The Best Day

Emma's Hilarious Horse Book (personalized for boys or girls with cats, dogs, penguins or frogs)
Emma, the Super, Amazing, Awesome, Intelligent, Girly-Girl (personalized)
Noah the Basketball Star (personalized for several sports for boys or girls)
Noah's Very Own Cook Book (personalized for boys or girls)
Grandma and Grandpa Love Emma (personalized from any relative for boys or girls)
Emma Turns One! (personalized for boys or girls ages 1-6)   and many more....

website: www.sneakysnailstories.com   facebook: Sneaky Snail Stories
Etsy: (search for) thesneakysnailstore   Amazon: (search for) Sally Helmick North

The Best Day!

written and illustrated by Sally Helmick North

Grandma and Grandpa Love You!

written and illustrated by Sally Helmick North

No Cookies for Kitty!

written and illustrated by Sally Helmick North

Your Aunt Loves You!

by Sally Helmick North

Made in the USA
Lexington, KY
02 January 2018